This book belongs to

.....Kaitlynn.........
Kirsty
.........Little.............

Publishing

www.gwpublishing.com

Hamish

This is Hamish the haggis
of the McHaggis clan,
rarely seen by
the eyes of man

Rupert Harold the Third
is an English gent,
travelling far from
his home in Kent

Rupert

Our Jeannie's an osprey with wide sweeping wings,
who is easily distracted by all sorts of things

Jeannie

Angus

Young Angus is cheeky and likes playing the fool,
What ever he's doing, he's got to look cool

For Dad
with love. L.S.

For Tessa
with love. S.J.C.

Text and Illustrations copyright © Linda Strachan and Sally J. Collins

www.lindastrachan.com

First Published in paperback in Great Britain 2005
Reprinted 2007

Design - Kevin Jeffery

Reprographics - GWP Graphics

Printing - Printer Trento, Italy

Published by

GW Publishing
PO Box 6091
Thatcham
Berks
RG19 8XZ

Tel +44 (0) 1635 268080

ISBN 09546701-8-3
978-0-9546701-8-4

Hamish McHaggis
and
The Skye Surprise

By Linda Strachan
Illustrated by Sally J. Collins

It was a lovely morning in Coorie
Doon and Hamish McHaggis was out
looking for heather nuts when he
stopped and looked up at the sky.

"She's back!" he shouted, rushing down to
the Hoggle to tell everyone the news.
"What's the matter?" yawned Rupert.
"What's all the fuss about?"
"It's Jeannie," Hamish said with a wide grin.
"She's back from Africa!"

Angus came racing down his favourite tree. "Jeannie! It's great to see you."

"Ouch! Aah! Ooch!" Jeannie yelped, as she
skid-landed on the heather covered hillside.
"I'd forgotten how jaggy this heather was."
"Wow! That was a stoater of a landing,
Jeannie," giggled Angus.

Jeannie had brought
back presents for
everyone,

an African Kora
for Rupert to play,

a new basket
for Hamish,

a drum and a
stick for Angus.

She had a special present for her
brother. "He's going to have
a surprise birthday
party," she told
them.

Jeannie's brother lived on the Isle of Skye and it wasn't long before she had to get ready to fly off again. Jeannie was packing all her brother's birthday presents into her travelling net.

"You'll not get all that in your net, Jeannie," Hamish said, shaking his head. "That's a muckle load. You'll never get off the ground."

"No, no. I'll be fine," Jeannie said, pushing another present into the bulging net.

"So, where exactly is Skye?" asked Angus, peering at the map.

"Right here, Angus," Rupert showed him. "And this is where Jeannie's brother lives."

When Jeannie had flown off on her way to Skye, Angus noticed a large parcel on the floor of the Hoggle.

He nudged it and the paper made a strange rustling noise. He poked at it again.

"I wonder what it is?" he muttered, poking it harder this time.

A piece of the wrapping paper tore open and Angus jumped back with a yelp. Two large, beady eyes stared back at him.

"Aargh! Help! Hamish, there's something in there!" he squealed.

Aargh!

"What's the matter, Angus?" Hamish puffed as he ran into the Hoggle.

"It . . . it's that . . . that thing!" Angus wailed. "It's got eyes!"

Angus, you shouldn't be opening that," Rupert frowned at him. "That's the present Jeannie brought back for her brother, she's left it behind."

"Jeannie will throw a stooshie if you've broken it,"
Hamish said. "I think we'd better wrap it up again."

"Perhaps we should just get into the Whirry-Bang
and take it to Skye for her," Rupert suggested. "I'd
like to go to Skye."

Jeannie was flying as fast as she could.
She was in a hurry to see her brother. She
flew over the hills, past Eilean Donan Castle
and on towards Skye. She was flying so fast
she didn't notice that her net had a tear in it.

First one thing dropped out . . .

and then another . . .

and another . . .

until the net was completely empty.

When Jeannie landed she saw the empty net.

"Oh no!" she wailed. "Everything's gone, even your special present."

"Don't cry Jeannie," her brother said, patting her with his wing.

Dunvegan Castle

"I know," she sniffed, "I'll fly back right now and maybe I can find the things I dropped."

Jeannie had just flown back over the Skye
bridge when she spotted the Whirry-Bang.

"Hamish! What are you doing here?"

"You left your brother's present behind so
we thought we'd bring it along for you," Hamish
grinned. "We found some other things, too."

Jeannie couldn't believe her eyes. They had found all the presents that had dropped out of her travelling net.

"Joe will be so pleased when he gets his presents," Jeannie told them. "You must all come and meet him."

When they arrived Jeannie's brother was delighted to
see them. "Fàilte," he said. "It means 'Welcome' in Gaelic."
"Happy Birthday, Joe," said Rupert, getting out his
camera as Jeannie gave Joe his special present.

Angus was a little nervous. "Aren't you
going to open it?" he asked.
He watched closely as Joe started to
unwrap his present . . .

Angus laughed when he saw Joe's present. It wasn't so scary after all.

"It's a bird! It's just a bird," he giggled, tapping it on the beak. "It's made of wood!"

HAPPY B
LA BREIT

Jeannie had another surprise for Joe.
"We're going to have a party,"
she told him. "Happy Birthday, Joe!"

Everyone joined in

HAPPY BIRTHDAY, JOE!

Joe was delighted. "This is the best
birthday surprise of all," he chirped.

DID YOU KNOW?

Coorie Doon means to nestle or cosy down comfortably

Blether means to gossip or chatter

A **stoater** means something outstanding or exceptional

A **muckle load** means a big or heavy load

To **throw a stooshie** means to cause a row or throw a tantrum

Fàlte means 'Welcome' in Gaelic

Là Breith Sona means 'Happy Birthday' in Gaelic

It is commonly thought that a **Haggis** has three legs, two long and one short. Hamish thinks this is hilarious

Angus is a Pine Marten

A **Pine Marten**'s lair is usually a hollow tree or a large crevice in a rock, lined with soft grass

Ospreys can have a wingspan of 4.5 ft.

Ospreys are sometimes known as Fish Hawks

Hedgehogs swim well and can even climb trees

On the **Isle of Skye** are the largest dinosaur footprints ever found in Scotland

A **Kora** is a harp-like instrument

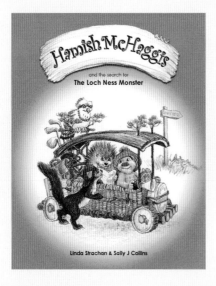

Hamish McHaggis and The Search for The Loch Ness Monster

Rupert doesn't believe in the Loch Ness Monster,
so Hamish and his friends take him to find Nessie.

09546701-5-9

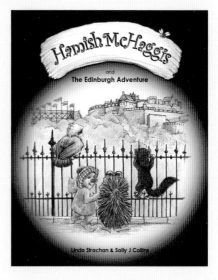

Hamish McHaggis and The Edinburgh Adventure

Hamish has tickets for the Tattoo at
Edinburgh Castle, but will they make it?

09546701-7-5

Hamish McHaggis and The Ghost of Glamis

Angus hears scary noises when they visit Hamish's
grandfather at Glamis Castle, could it be a ghost?

09546701-9-1

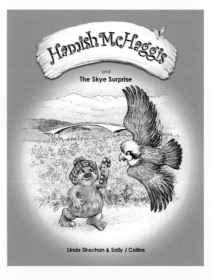

Hamish McHaggis and The Skye Surprise

Jeannie's brother is having a surprise party on the Isle
of Skye, but he's not the only one who gets a surprise.

09546701-8-3